# FIONA
## Helps a Friend

NEW YORK TIMES BESTSELLING ILLUSTRATOR
**R I C H A R D   C O W D R E Y**

**Z** | ZONDER**kidz**

*"To my best friend John (Barney)."*
—RC

ZONDERKIDZ

*Fiona Helps a Friend*
Copyright © 2021 by Zondervan
Illustrations © 2021 by Zondervan

Requests for information
should be addressed to:

Zonderkidz, 3900 Sparks Dr. SE,
Grand Rapids, Michigan 49546

*Illustrated by: Richard Cowdrey*
*Contributors: Barbara Herndon and Mary Hassinger*
*Art direction and design: Cindy Davis*

*Printed in Korea*

21 22 23 24 25 /SAM/ 20 19 18 17 16 15 14 13 12 11 10 9 8 7 6 5 4 3 2 1

It was another warm day at the zoo. As Fiona wandered around saying hello to her animal friends, she wondered, *Why is the zoo so quiet today?*

GRUNT
GRUNT

GR

Co

twweeettt

There were the usual GRUNTS and GROWLS, CHIRPS and CHATTER … but something was missing.
Suddenly Fiona realized she hadn't heard Matilda the Kookaburra's laugh all day!

Fiona asked her friend Giraffe, "Have you heard Matilda today?"
"No, I haven't," he said. "But I did hear she's been feeling a little blue."

OOWWL

chirp
chirp

OOOO
OOOOO

"We need to go over there and cheer her up. C'mon, everyone!"
Fiona let out a snort, wiggled her ears, and said, "We've got this!"

Fiona and her friends marched over
to the bird house to see Matilda.

"Hi, Matilda! We missed you today!"
Fiona said, as her friends jumped in
trying to make the Kookaburra laugh.

"Matilda! Watch this!" called Monkey as he swung on a high branch, doing flips and making funny faces.

"Look, over here!" the animals called to Matilda
as they all did their best, funniest moves
to try and make the kookaburra laugh!

They even made their silliest faces.
But Matilda didn't crack a smile.

"Thank you for coming to visit," she said. Then Matilda politely excused herself and hopped back inside her house.

Elephant let out a sigh and said, "I think Matilda has lost her laugh."

"Then we're just going to have to help her find it!" shouted the spunky little hippo.

Fiona and her friends searched
the zoo high and low,
looking for just the right thing
to make Matilda laugh.

Just as the animals were about to give up, a golf cart came zooming around the corner.
As it flew past, it hit a bump and a big brown box bounced off the back and landed on the path.

# LOST + FOUND

Fiona wandered over to get a closer look.
"What's a LOST AND FOUND?" she asked.

"Sometimes people lose things," explained Elephant. "When the zookeepers find those lost things,
they put them in a box to keep them safe. Then people can come back and get them."

Fiona had a thought. Maybe Matilda's laugh was in the LOST AND FOUND!
Everyone agreed it was the perfect place to look.

"Wow! Look at all this fun stuff!" cried Fiona as she put on a funny-looking hat. "Howdy, partner!" Cheetah tried to run in a pair of sneakers. "Zoom, zoooom!"

Ostrich found bright
red sunglasses.
"I'm a movie star."

As they went through the box the animals giggled and gasped,
trying things on. They never had a dress-up party before!

As the friends laughed at one another and showed off their costumes,
Fiona suddenly realized they had forgotten all about Matilda! They were so busy
having fun themselves, they forgot to look for the Kookaburra's laugh!

Just then, a big smile came
over Fiona's face.

The little hippo let out a snort, wiggled her ears, and said, "I've got this!
I think THIS is going to help Matilda find her laugh!"

Fiona and her animal dress-up
party made their way back to Matilda.
"Come out, Matilda. We have something for you."
Matilda came out to see.

Fiona slid a huge bowtie and a pair of silly glasses onto the sad bird.

Monkey held up a little mirror so Matilda could see.

Then everyone heard it.
It started as a quiet chuckle.
Then the sound got louder and louder until ...

SCREEEEEEEEEEEEECH!

WHAHAHAHA

HOOOOOWL

ROAR

... it turned into the biggest belly laugh
the animals had ever heard!

Matilda's laugh rang through the air! The animals
in the zoo ROARED, HOWLED, SCREECHED, and SQUAWKED
in celebration. And it was music to Fiona's ears.

Grrrrrr...rr

Later that night, as Fiona snuggled up for bed, she told Mama about her day and how she and her friends helped Matilda find her laugh.

Mama smiled sweetly at her little hippo.

"You are a good friend, Fiona. Now WHY DON'T WE ALL try to quiet down and go to sleep."

SQWAHAHAHA

And Fiona did.